Tiger
on a Tree

Anushka Ravishankar

Pulak Biswas

Tiger, tiger

on the shore

Does he want

to go across?

Make a dash?

Be bold? Be rash?

splash!

Tiger, tiger,

going far

Baaaaaaaa

aaah!

This tree is the

Tiger! Tiger?

On a tree!

Tiger? On a tree?

Rubbish! Cannot be

It's true! I saw it too!

Now what to do?

Tie him tight!

shoo him!

Boo him!

Make him jump!

Dum duma dum dum

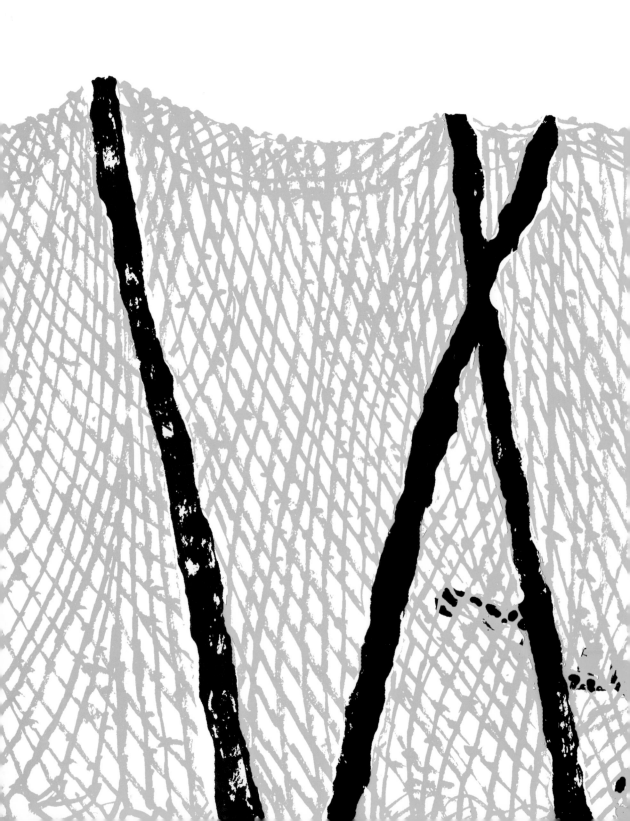

Thump.

He's caught.

He's got.

Now what?

Stick him up with glue?

Paint him an electric blue?

I know, set him free.

Free???

So.

Tiger, tiger on the shore

TIGER ON A TREE
Copyright © 1997

For the text: Anushka Ravishankar
For the illustrations: Pulak Biswas

For this edition: Tara Books, India, *tarabooks.com*
and Tara Publishing Ltd., UK, *tarabooks.com/uk*

First printing 1997. Second printing 2002.
Third printing 2004. Fourth printing 2007.
This edition 2013

Design and typography: Rathna Ramanathan, *m9design.com*
Production: C. Arumugam
Printed in India by Sudarsan Graphics Pvt. Ltd.

ISBN 978-93-83145-06-5